FLASH THE DONKEY
Makes New Friends

Written and Illustrated by RACHEL ANNE RIDGE

TYNDALE®
MOMENTUM

An Imprint of
Tyndale House Publishers, Inc.

CHAPTER 1
MEETING

Some adventures begin with
"Once upon a time . . ."

But mine begins with
an old blue wagon and a good idea.

1

I found the wagon on my travels.

See, I like to go from town to town
and place to place.

It's nice to sleep anywhere you want.

Most of the time.

Well, some of the time.

The wagon was in bad shape,
but the wheels still turned.

I decided to fill it up with interesting stuff.

This was my good idea.

I looked here and there, high and low.

If something caught my eye or looked useful, I put it in the wagon.

Soon my wagon was piled high with treasures.

So high. Too high!

Now it was heavy.

So heavy. Too heavy!

URRUGH!

4

Suddenly I could not pull my wagon anymore.
My wagon pulled ME!

Down a hill I tumbled.

Down,
down,
down!

But I held on . . .

. . . until a tree **jumped** in front of me!

6

CRASH!

Now my idea did not seem like
a good one at all.

7

"What is it?" chirped a voice.

"I don't kno-o-o-w," said another voice.

"It's a unicorn!" shouted a third, with an oink.

I opened my eyes wide.

Three sets of eyes looked back at me.

"That's not a unicorn,"
said the chirpy voice.
Her small eyes sparkled.
"That's a donkey with a giant lump on his head!"

9

Feathers brushed my forehead.

"OUCH!"

"We must take him to his home,"
the third voice said.

My head hurt even more.
"I don't have a home. I'm on my own."

10

The three of them looked at one another.

"Let's put his things back in the wagon. He will come with us."

The chicken was clearly in charge.

Suddenly my idea was a good one again.

CHAPTER 2
CARING

"I'm Ruby," said the chicken. "Sit here."
Ruby gave me some ice for my lump. I liked her right away.

"Will he get pajamas?"
asked the goat, whose name was Jed.

"We will see," said Ruby.

"Ahem," said the pig. "I'm Carson. And you must be . . . ?"

SEEDS

"Very tired," I said with a yawn. I looked around. Beds!

One of them looked especially nice.

"Maybe he's not very smart—he piled his wagon w-a-a-a-y too high,"
Jed whispered to Carson.

"I can hear you," I said.

"My ears work just fine."

I wiggled them up and down.

"And everyone just calls me Donkey,"
I added.

"Let's get you tucked in, Donkey,"
      clucked Ruby, helping me to the nice bed.

            Carson brought me a cup of tea on a tray.
"This will help you sleep tight," he said,

"so you can be on the road again tomorrow."

16

Jed harrumphed, then bounded up a tower of hay bales.
"Piled his wagon w-a-a-ay too high,"
he muttered.

I noticed that no one
mentioned pajamas again.

CORN

In the morning, Ruby woke me with news:

"Sorry to disturb you, but we have a PROBLEM."

Jed blurted out, "Today is our Annual Neighborhood Pancake Breakfast,
and we are in charge of making the pancakes."

This did not seem like a problem to me.
Pancakes sounded delicious, and I was quite hungry.

"But our pancake machine is broken," moaned Carson.
He wiped his forehead.
"How are we going to make the pancakes now?"

"This is a DIS-A-A-A-STER!"
Jed shouted.

Ruby began to cry.

"I have an idea,"
I said.
"Where is my wagon?
I might have something useful in there."

RITTLE-RATTLE-CLACK-CLACK.

Jed pulled the blue wagon full of treasures next to me.

"Shall we look at the pancake machine?" I asked.

"Right this way," said Jed.

"Oh," I said. "It's grand!"

I tapped some parts and wiggled others. Then I went to work.

"Wire, please."

"Spring."

"Chain."

FLOUR

22

Carson closed his eyes.

"It's too late!" he cried.
"The neighbors are starting to arrive!"

Ruby fanned his face.

"Almost done," I said.

"I'll have this finished in a flash."

The last piece snapped into place.

"Now let's see if this works!"

BANG! SQUEAK! POP!
CLICKETY-CLACK! WHIRRR!

"Get the milk! Grab the flour!" Ruby flapped into action.
"We're in business."

All the neighbors cheered.

"MOO!"

"cluck!"

"baaa!"

"meow!"

"NEIGH!"

If I say so myself,
the Annual Neighborhood
Pancake Breakfast
was a smashing...

success!

"Well, I must be going now," I said.

I put my things back in the wagon.

"Perhaps you should have some tea first, Donkey," said Carson.

"That bump on your head still needs some attention," said Ruby.

"And my bicycle is making a funny sound. Will you take a look?" Jed asked.

Three sets of eyes
looked at me.

I thought for a moment. "I could stay a little longer," I said.

Jed clapped and Carson put the teakettle on.

"How do you feel about pajamas?" Ruby cocked her head.

"I think I might like flannel," I smiled.

EGGS

If you have never been invited to a Pajama Ceremony, let me tell you what happens.
First, a goat plays a ukulele and sings a special song.

Then, a chicken steps forward to present you with flannel pajamas, which are very soft.

32

Finally,
a pig recites a poem.
"Ahem . . ."

Your adventure began with
a dash.
Then a tree caused your wagon
to crash.
But you saved the day,
quickly finding a way,
and now we shall call you

OUR FLASH!

"Y-a-a-a-a-y!"

shouted Jed, leaping onto the table.

Carson bowed,
letting out a small squeal,
and Ruby cackled with glee.

34

But all I heard was,

"And now we shall call you our Flash."

If you have never been to a
Pajama PARTY,
well . . . this is what comes
after the Pajama Ceremony . . .

There is cake, music, and
dancing. There is popcorn,
storytelling, and fun.

And at the end of the party, you fall asleep in an especially nice bed
... one with your very own name on it.

FLASH

The seeds
of good deeds
become a tree of life;
a wise person
wins friends.

PROVERBS 11:30

Now That You've Finished the Story . . .

Who are your friends?

Write their names on the hay bales (or have a parent help you).

As we discovered, Ruby, Carson, Jed, and Flash became caring friends to one another.

How do you and your friends care for one another?

_____

_____

_____

_____

_____

The Bible says that "the seeds of good deeds become a tree of life" and that "a wise person wins friends." Doing good deeds is a way to help someone in need. By helping one another, Ruby, Carson, Jed, and Flash became good friends.

What are some ways you can help others and make friends? Here are some good ideas.

- Invite someone to play with you.

- Let others go first in line.

- Make a card for someone who is sick or needs cheering up.

- Help someone who is having a hard time with a chore or task.

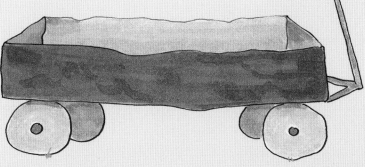

About the Author

Rachel Anne Ridge wrote the story and painted all the pictures you see in this book. She lives in Texas and adopted an actual stray donkey she named Flash and his miniature donkey friend, Henry.

The heartwarming true tale of an irrepressible donkey
who needed a home—and forever changed a family.

RACHEL ANNE
RIDGE

Readers will be clamoring for more of Flash . . . powerful and uplifting.
PUBLISHERS WEEKLY

The Homeless
Donkey Who
Taught Me about
Life, Faith, and
Second Chances

Flash

Foreword by
Priscilla Shirer

978-1-4143-9784-9

When Rachel Anne Ridge discovered a wounded, frightened donkey standing in her driveway, she couldn't turn him away. And against all odds, he turned out to be the very thing her family needed most. They let him into their hearts . . . and he taught them things they never knew about life, love, and faith.

Prepare to fall in love with Flash: a quirky, unlikely hero with gigantic ears, a deafening bray, a personality as big as Texas, and a story you'll never forget.

Available everywhere books are sold.

CP1098

Visit Tyndale's website for kids at www.tyndale.com/kids.

Tyndale Momentum and the Tyndale Momentum logo are registered trademarks of Tyndale House Publishers, Inc. Tyndale Momentum is an imprint of Tyndale House Publishers, Inc., Carol Stream, Illinois.

Flash the Donkey Makes New Friends

Designed by Jennifer Phelps

Edited by Bonne Steffen

Published in association with the literary agency of William K. Jensen Literary Agency, 119 Bampton Court, Eugene, OR 97404.

All Scripture quotations are taken from the *Holy Bible*, New Living Translation, copyright © 1996, 2004, 2007, 2015 by Tyndale House Foundation. Used by permission of Tyndale House Publishers, Inc., Carol Stream, Illinois 60188. All rights reserved.

For manufacturing information regarding this product, please call 1-800-323-9400.

Library of Congress Cataloging-in-Publication Data
Names: Ridge, Rachel Anne, author.
Title: Flash the Donkey makes new friends / Rachel Anne Ridge.
Description: Carol Stream, IL : Tyndale House Publishers, Inc., 2016.
Identifiers: LCCN 2016001964 | ISBN 9781496413956 (hc)
Subjects: LCSH: Conduct of life--Juvenile literature. | Christian children--Conduct of life--Juvenile literature.
Classification: LCC BJ1631 .R48 2016 | DDC 177/.62--dc23 LC record available at https://lccn.loc.gov/2016001964

Printed in China

22	21	20	19	18	17	16
7	6	5	4	3	2	1

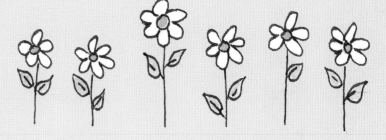